My Weird School Special

Oh, Valentine, We've Lost Our Minds!

Dan Gutman

Pictures by

Jim Paillot

ST. JOHN THE BAPTIST PARISH LIBRARY
2920 NEW HIGHWAY 51
LAPLACE, LOUISIANA 70068

HARPER

An Imprint of HarperCollins*Publishers*

To Emma

My Weird School Special: Oh, Valentine, We've Lost Our Minds!

For information address HarperCollins Children's Books, a division of HarperCollins Publishers, 195 Broadway, New York, NY 10007.

www.harpercollinschildrens.com

Library of Congress Cataloging-in-Publication Data

Gutman, Dan.

Oh, Valentine, we've lost our minds! / Dan Gutman ; pictures by Jim Paillot. – First edition.

pages cm – (My weird school special)

Summary: "Prepare for weirdness when Ella Mentry School gets a French foreign exchange student just in time for Valentine's Day!"– Provided by publisher.

ISBN 978-0-06-228403-7 (pbk. bdg.) – ISBN 978-0-06-228404-4 (lib. bdg.)

[1. Schools–Fiction. 2. Foreign study–Fiction. 3. Valentine's Day–Fiction. 4. Teachers–Fiction. 5. Humorous stories.] I. Title.

PZ7.G9846Oh 2014 2014013834

[Fic]–dc23 CIP

AC

Typography by Kate J. Engbring

14 15 16 17 18 OPM 10 9 8 7 6 5 4 3 2 1

❖

First Edition

Contents

CAMP OCKATOLLYQUAY
Tests aRe fun!

A.J.
RYAN
MICHAEL
A
ANDREA
EMILY
NEIL

LOVE
A+

Word of the Week

My name is A.J. and I hate the *L* word.

Do you know what the *L* word is? I can't say it. It's too gross.

We had just finished putting our back-packs into our cubbies and pledging the allegiance when my teacher, Mr. Granite, went over to the whiteboard.

"It's time for our Word of the Day," he

said as he picked up a marker. "Today, our word is . . ."

And then he wrote it on the board in big letters: L-O-V-E.

"Love," said Mr. Granite.

WHAT?!

He said the *L* word! Ugh, disgusting!

"Yuck!" shouted Ryan, who will eat anything, even stuff that isn't food.

"That's a four-letter word!" shouted Michael, who never ties his shoes.

"And he said it *out loud*!" shouted Neil, who we call the nude kid even though he wears clothes.

"Yes, tomorrow is Valentine's Day," said Mr. Granite. "The day of *love*."

He said it *again*! All of us guys were

falling off our chairs and choking and gagging and freaking out.

"Boys!" said Andrea Young, this girl who is always rolling her eyes.* "I *love* Valentine's Day!"

"Me too!" said her crybaby friend, Emily, who agrees with everything Andrea says. "I *love* Valentine's Day!"

"Can I go to the nurse?" I asked Mr. Granite. "I think I'm gonna be sick."

"What's the matter, A.J.?"

"Everybody keeps saying the *L* word," I told him.

"You mean 'love'?" asked Mr. Granite.

"Ewwwww!" I shouted. "You said it

---

*If you roll your eyes too much, they roll right out of your head. That's a fact.

again! Help! Call an ambulance! I need to go to the hospital!"

"You're being silly, A.J.," Mr. Granite told me. "I bet you love *lots* of things."

"Oh, yeah? Name one."

"You love your parents, don't you?" asked Mr. Granite.

"Well, yes," I admitted.

Of course I love my parents.

"And I've heard you say how much you

love skateboarding, right?"

"I guess so," I admitted.

"And I *know* how much you love playing Pee Wee football every Saturday, A.J.," said Mr. Granite.

"Yeah . . ."

I couldn't argue with *that.* I do love playing football.

"So there are some things that you love."

Hmmm. Mr. Granite had a point. I do love my parents, skateboarding, and football. But I still don't like the *L* word.

Mr. Granite told us that the *L* word is also about tolerance and acceptance and peace in the world. That's what we should celebrate on Valentine's Day.

"I'll tell you what is my favorite part

about Valentine's Day," said Mr. Granite. "Getting chocolate."

CHOCOLATE?!

If there's one thing that I *really* love, it's chocolate. I think I love chocolate more than anything in the whole world. I guess I can put up with some of that mushy *L*-word stuff if there's the chance that I might be getting chocolate.

"Valentine's Day is going to be fun!" Mr. Granite told us. "We're going to have a party. But for now let's get to work. I know another thing you all love—math! So turn to page twenty-three in your—"

Mr. Granite never had the chance to finish his sentence. Because you'll never believe in a million hundred years who walked into the door at that moment.

Nobody! It would hurt if you walked into a door. But you'll never believe who walked into the door*way*.

I'm not going to tell you.

Okay, okay, I'll tell you. But you have to read the next chapter. So nah-nah-nah boo-boo on you.

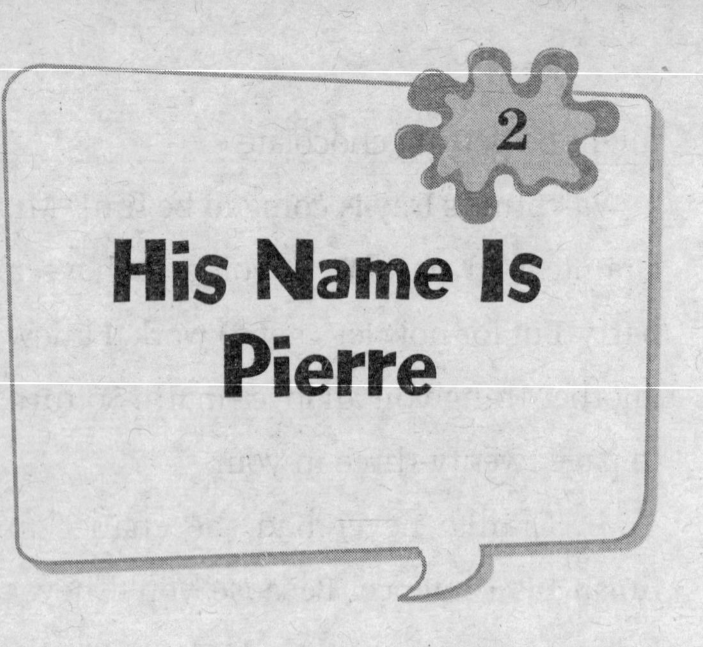

2 His Name Is Pierre

It was our principal, Mr. Klutz!

He has no hair at all. I mean *none.* I wonder if hats slip off his head because they have nothing to hold on to.

"Mr. Klutz!" said Mr. Granite. "To what do we owe the pleasure of your company?"

(That's grown-up talk for "What are *you* doing here?")

"I have big news!" Mr. Klutz announced.

"He has a big nose," I whispered to Ryan.

Everybody was buzzing because we were going to get some big news. Mr. Klutz held up his hand and made a peace sign with his fingers, which means "shut up."

"Guess what, kids?" said Mr. Klutz. "Your class is going to get an exchange student!"

Exchange student? What's *that*?

I raised my hand, and Mr. Klutz called on me.

"Does that mean we can exchange one of our students for something else?" I asked. "I say we exchange Andrea for a video game system."

"Oh, snap!" said Ryan.

Andrea rolled her eyes.

"An exchange student is a boy or girl from a foreign country, Arlo," she said. Andrea calls me by my real name because she knows I don't like it.

"I knew that," I lied.

"What country does our exchange student come from?" Mr. Granite asked.

"He came all the way from France," said Mr. Klutz. "His name is Pierre."

Pee Air?

Mr. Klutz *had* to be joking. We all started giggling and poking each other with our elbows.

"Did his parents name him Pee Air because he peed in the air?" I asked. "My mom told me that when I was a baby, I used to pee in the air while she was changing my diaper."

"That's disgusting, Arlo!" said Andrea. "We're not supposed to talk about things like that in school."

"Can you possibly be more boring?" I asked her.

Mr. Klutz went into the hallway to get the French kid named Pee Air. He was out there for a long time. I wondered what Pee Air would be like. We were all glued to our seats.

Well, not really. That would be weird. Why would anybody glue themselves to a seat? How would you get the glue off?

Mr. Klutz came back into the classroom with Pee Air. Pee Air was holding a big platter, which he put on a table at the front of the room.

"Pee Air," said Mr. Klutz, "I would like to introduce you to Mr. Granite's third-grade class."

"O-M-G!" whispered Andrea. "Pee Air is *handsome*!"

"He's *adorable*!" whispered Emily.

All the girls were swooning and giggling and fanning themselves and making goo-goo eyes at Pee Air. Even my friend Alexia, who is a tomboy, was freaking out.

"He's *dreamy*!" Alexia said.

Pee Air did one of those deep bows like actors do at the end of a play.

"Bonjour," he said.

"Ooooh!" said Andrea. "He's handsome, *and* he speaks *French*!"

Well of *course* Pee Air speaks French.

He's from France! *Everybody* in France speaks French. What is Andrea's problem?

"Pee Air, I have to go to a meeting," Mr. Klutz said, "but I'll be back later to see how you're making out."

Ewww, disgusting!

"We," said Pee Air.

"We means 'yes' in French," said Andrea, who thinks she knows everything. "They spell it O-U-I."

That's weird. And I thought *I* was a bad speller. Those people in France totally don't know how to spell.

Mr. Granite went into the hallway to talk with Mr. Klutz. So we were alone with Pee Air.

"I am very happy . . . to be in your . . . classroom," Pee Air told us. "I am just learning how to speak English . . . at my school, but I am not very . . . good at it yet."

He said it all in a weird French accent. The girls were still making goo-goo eyes at him.

Pee Air continued. . . .

"So I hope you will . . . how do you say . . . bear with me."

"Bare with you?" I shouted. "I'm not taking my clothes off in school. Gross!"

"Not B-A-R-E, Arlo!" said Andrea. "B-E-A-R! Pee Air said 'bear with me.'"

"There's a bear with him?" I shouted. "Where?"

"Run for your lives!" shouted Neil the nude kid. "Pee Air has a bear!"

I hid under my desk. I didn't see any bears around, but you can't be too careful these days. For all I know, kids in France bring bears to school with them.

Andrea got up from her desk and ran over to Pee Air.

"My name is Andrea," she said, doing one of those girly curtsy things. "It's a pleasure to meet you, Pee Air."

That's when the most amazing thing in the history of the world happened. Pee Air took Andrea's hand and *kissed* it!

Ugh, gross!

I would *never* kiss anybody's hand,

and certainly not Andrea's. Hands are dirty. You don't know *where* that hand has been. There was a fifty-fifty chance that Andrea used that hand to pick her nose.

"The pleasure is all mine, Andrea," Pee Air said. "Your eyes . . . are like pools of water . . . in the moonlight."

What a dork.

Pee Air held on to Andrea's hand way too long. Andrea was giggling and blushing as she ran back to her seat.

Then Emily got up and went over to Pee Air.

"I'm Emily," she said, all giggly. "Welcome to our class, Pee Air."

Pee Air kissed Emily's hand, too.

"Your face . . . is like an angel's," he said. "I hope that we might . . . become better acquainted."

Emily was giggling and blushing as she ran back to her seat.

After that, all the other girls in the class went running up to introduce themselves and get their hands kissed by Pee Air. Even Alexia! I thought I was gonna throw up.

"I'm never going to wash this hand again!" Alexia said when she went back to her seat.

There was no way I was going to go up and introduce myself to Pee Air. I didn't want him slobbering all over my hand like a dog.

Mr. Granite came back into the classroom and went to his desk.

"Mr. Klutz told me that Pee Air will be with us for the rest of the week."

The rest of the week! That's like *forever.*

"How many days are there in a French week?" I asked.

"Seven," said Mr. Granite.

Wow. Just like here.

"It's already Wednesday," Andrea said. "So Pee Air will only be here for three days."

"I brought a little . . . how do you say . . . gift . . . from my home," Pee Air announced.

Hmm. I like gifts. Maybe Pee Air wasn't such a bad guy after all. He picked up the platter he had brought with him.

"It is cheese and crackers," said Pee Air.

WHAT?!

Cheese and crackers? *That's* a gift? I thought he was going to give us something cool from France, like French fries or French toast. Who shows up at a new school with a platter full of cheese?

"What kind of cheese is it, Pee Air?" asked Mr. Granite.

"It is called Muenster cheese," said Pee Air.

Muenster cheese? My dad told me he used to watch a TV show about that cheese when he was a kid.*

"We have over four hundred kinds of cheeses in France," said Pee Air.

Four *hundred*? Those French people should make up their minds. The only kind of cheese I eat is American cheese. Each slice is wrapped up in its own piece of plastic, so you know it's good.

Pee Air walked around the room with his platter of cheese. It wasn't wrapped up in plastic. It was cut into little chunks, and each one had a toothpick sticking out of it. That was weird.

Some of the kids tried a piece of cheese. When Pee Air got to me with the platter, I

---

*www.youtube.com/watch?v=PLnYLVP5fi0

leaned over to sniff the cheese.

Gross! It was stinky! I guess they have toothpicks so you can use them to get the smell out of your mouth after eating the cheese.

"Ugh, it smells horrible," I said. "Who

cut the cheese?"

"Very funny, Arlo," said Andrea, rolling her eyes again.

Why can't a truck full of cheese fall on Andrea's head?

That French cheese was gross. No way was I going to eat that stuff. It smelled like it was sitting out in the hot sun all day. I wasn't going to shake hands with Pee Air, and I wasn't going to eat his stinky cheese either. That guy is weird.

3

A Teachable Moment

After Pee Air passed around his stinky cheese, Mr. Granite told us to open up our math books again. But you'll never believe who poked her head into the door at that moment.

Nobody! Why would anybody want to poke their head into a door? I thought we went over that already in chapter one. But you'll never believe who poked her head into the door*way*.

It was Ms. LaGrange, our school lunch lady! She was wearing an apron and a chef's hat. Ms. LaGrange is from France, just like Pee Air.

"Bonjour!" said Ms. LaGrange. "I heard your class has a new exchange student from France."

"His name is Pee Air," said Alexia.

"Blah blah blah blah," Ms. LaGrange said to Pee Air. "Blah blah blah blah."

"Blah blah blah blah," Pee Air said to Ms. LaGrange. "Blah blah blah blah."

I had no idea what they were saying,

because they were talking to each other in French. It made no sense at all. I don't know how anybody understands that stuff.

"Isn't French a *beautiful* language?" said Andrea. "When I get older, I'm going to take a class and learn how to speak French."

"Me too," said Emily, who always does everything Andrea does.

"This is what I call a teachable moment!" said Mr. Granite as he put down his math book. "It's the perfect time for us to learn about another country!"

"Yay!" shouted all the girls.

"Boo!" shouted all the boys.

Learning stuff is boring.

"What would you like to know about France?" asked Ms. LaGrange. "I'm sure Pee Air and I can answer any questions."

Andrea started waving her hand in the air like she was stranded on a desert island and trying to signal a plane. So of course Ms. LaGrange called on her.

"Is it true that the French people gave us the Statue of Liberty?" Andrea asked.

"Yes!" said Ms. LaGrange. "The Statue of Liberty was a gift from France."

"Very good, Andrea!" said Mr. Granite.

Little Miss Know-It-All had a big smile on her face. What a brownnoser! She knew perfectly well that the French people gave us the Statue of Liberty. She only asked that question so everybody would *know* that she knew the French people gave us the Statue of Liberty.

Andrea is always doing that.

"How big is France?" asked Alexia.

"France is about the same size as Texas," said Ms. LaGrange.

"WOW," everybody said, which is "MOM" upside down.

"Did you ever go to the Eiffel Tower?" asked Michael.

"Oh yes, many times," said Pee Air. "It is very . . . how do you say . . . cool."

"The *Mona Lisa* is in France too," said Andrea, who was obviously trying to impress Pee Air with how much she knows.

"Very good, Andrea!" said Mr. Granite.

Why can't a truck full of *Mona Lisa*s

fall on Andrea's head?

"Hey," I asked, "in France, do you call French fries 'American fries'?"

"No, we call them *pommes frites*," said Pee Air. "We also eat . . . frogs' legs and snails . . . which we call escargot."

Ewww, gross! They eat snails!

"Maybe I'll make escargot for lunch tomorrow!" said Ms. LaGrange.

Ugh! I'll be bringing my own lunch. I'd rather die than eat those S car things.

"Did you know that the hot air balloon, the parachute, and the submarine were all invented in France?" asked Ms. LaGrange.

"They probably invented that stuff so they could get out of the country," I said.

"Why would they want to get out of the country, A.J.?" asked Mr. Granite.

"So they won't have to eat frogs' legs, snails, and stinky cheese anymore," I said.

"Oh, snap!" said Ryan.

"Very funny, Arlo," said Andrea.

"Do you have Valentine's Day in France?" asked Emily.

"Oh yes," said Pee Air. "But in France, *every* day is Valentine's Day."

Ugh, gross.

"There are lots of English words that come from French," said Little Miss Perfect. "Like 'souvenir' and 'mayonnaise.'"

"And 'villain,' 'dungeon,' 'rendezvous,' and 'camouflage,'" added Ms. LaGrange.

"And 'croissant,' 'turquoise,' 'cinema,' and 'aviation,'" added Pee Air.

"And 'thermometer,' 'leotard,' 'garage,' and 'machine,'" added Mr. Granite.

Blah blah blah blah. What a snoozefest.

I thought I was gonna die from old age.

We learned a lot of stuff about France from Pee Air and Ms. LaGrange. Did you know that just twelve years after our Revolutionary War, they had a revolution in France? So they were just a bunch of copycats. We also learned about some French guy named Napoleon who was always sticking his hand in his shirt. Nobody knew why. I guess he had a rash or something.

That guy should get some ointment to put on his stomach.

Then Pee Air taught us a song called "Frère Jacques." It's about a guy who isn't sure if his brother is asleep or not. That song is weird. If my brother was lying there and I couldn't tell if he was asleep, I'd call an ambulance, not write some dumb song about it.

"We have certainly learned a lot about France this morning," said Mr. Granite. "But it's time to get back to our work now. Turn to page twenty-three in your math books, please."

That's when the weirdest thing in the history of the world happened.

*BRING! BRING! BRING!**

It was the lunch bell. We all cleared off our desks and got ready to go to lunch.

I learned one important thing about France: If you talk about France long enough, you don't have to do math.

---

*The lunch bell in my school sounds just like the word "bring." Nobody knows why.

4 Lunch with Pee Air

We walked in single file to the vomitorium. It used to be called the cafetorium, but then some first grader threw up in there and it's been the vomitorium ever since.

"Ooooh, sit next to me, Pee Air!" begged Andrea.

"No, sit next to *me*!" begged Alexia.

"Can I sit next to you, Pee Air?" begged Emily.

"I asked him first!" said Andrea.

All the girls were fighting over who would get to sit next to Pee Air. That's good. They wouldn't be bothering us at *our* table for a change.

"I will sit next to *all* of you . . . lovely ladies," said Pee Air. "Maybe you can . . . teach me some English."

"And maybe *you* can teach us some French," said Andrea, giggling.

The guys and I sat down at our table. The girls crowded around Pee Air at the next table.

"I hope I get to visit Paris someday," said Andrea, who was all goo-goo eyes. "It's *so* romantic!"

"Maybe I will . . . take you there someday, Andrea," said Pee Air.

"Oooooooooooo!" went all the girls. Andrea was all giggly and red faced.

We took out our lunches. We all watched as Pee Air opened his backpack. I was sure he was going to pull out a bunch of frogs' legs and snails and French onion soup and other stinky, gross stuff they eat in France.

"I have a baguette," Pee Air said.

"What's *that*?" I asked. "A little bag?"

But Pee Air pulled out this giant bread thing. It was like two feet long! I bet that thing is the longest bread in the history of the world. You could have a sword fight with that bread.

"WOW," everybody said, which is "MOM" upside down.

Pee Air also took out some more of his stinky cheese. He *never* runs out of that stuff. Pee Air broke off pieces of bread and cheese and handed them around to the girls.

The guys and I ate our lunch without saying anything. We were trying to listen to what they were saying at the next table.

"Pee Air, what is *this* called in French?" Andrea asked as she held up a piece of cheese.

"That is *fromage*," Pee Air replied. "'*Fromage*' is the French word for 'cheese.'"

"How do you say 'napkin'?" Emily asked, holding up her napkin.

"'*Serviette*,'" said Pee Air.

"How do you say 'fish'?" asked Alexia.

"'Fish' is '*poisson*,'" said Pee Air.

"That sounds like 'poison'!" all the girls said, giggling uncontrollably.

"Oh, Pee Air, you are simply *adorable*!" said Andrea.

The girls were all laughing their heads off even though Pee Air didn't say anything funny.

"I don't like Pee Air," I finally whispered to the guys.

"Me neither," said Michael.

"I think you're jealous of him, A.J.," whispered Neil the nude kid.

"Me? Jealous?" I said. "I'm not jealous of *him*."

Well, maybe I was a *little* jealous of Pee

Air. He was really handsome and he had a cool French accent and the girls were giving him all the attention.

"You're jealous that Andrea likes Pee Air," said Neil.

"I am not!" I said. "I can't stand Andrea."

"Ooooo!" Ryan said. "A.J. says he can't stand Andrea. They must be in *LOVE*!"

"When are you and Andrea gonna get married?" asked Michael.

If those guys weren't my best friends, I would hate them.

5 Girls Are Weird

After lunch we went out to the playground for recess. Michael grabbed a football, and we started throwing it back and forth.

"Hey, Pee Air!" yelled Ryan. "Wanna throw the football with us?"

"*Merci*, but no," said Pee Air. "I don't know . . . how to play."

"We can teach you," said Neil the nude kid.

"Play with *us*, Pee Air!" begged Andrea.

"Ooooh, yes!" begged all the girls. "Play with *us*! *Pleeeeeeze?*"

Pee Air ran over to the girls. They were playing hopscotch and jacks and jump rope and other girly games we refuse to

play. I kept looking over at the girls while we threw the football back and forth.

"You are *so* much fun, Pee Air!" Andrea shouted as she hopscotched. "The boys *never* want to play with us."

After we got tired of throwing the football around, me and the guys sat down on the grass to watch the girls playing with Pee Air.

"Look at that guy," I said. "He actually looks like he's having fun playing with the girls."

"And they're all making goo-goo eyes at him," said Ryan.

We watched Pee Air and Andrea go over to the swings together. That's when the most amazing thing in the history of the world happened. Pee Air took off his jacket!

Well, that's not the amazing part. I'm sure Pee Air takes off his jacket all the time. The amazing part was what he *did* with his jacket.

There was a puddle of water in front of one of the swings. After Pee Air took off his jacket, he put it down on the ground over the puddle! Right in the water! Then he made a deep bow, and Andrea stepped on the jacket to get to the swing.

WHAT?!

Me and the guys couldn't believe our eyes! Andrea could have just walked *around* the puddle to get to the swing. But Pee Air ruined a perfectly good jacket so Andrea wouldn't have to walk a couple of feet.

"Oh, Pee Air!" I heard Andrea say. "You are so gallant!"

I'm not sure, but I guess "gallant" means a guy who throws his clothes into puddles of water.

We all watched Andrea and Pee Air swing on the swings. They were talking to each other for a long time, but I couldn't hear what they were saying.

BRING! BRING! BRING!

Recess was over. We lined up to go back inside the school. All the girls ran over to Andrea.

"You won't believe what happened!" Andrea told them. "Pee Air just told me I am his *special* valentine!"

"Eeeeeek!" all the girls screamed.

"Not only that," Andrea said, "but he asked me to go out for ice cream with him after school today!"

"Eeeeeek!"

"You are the luckiest girl in the whole

world!" said Emily.

"I wish Pee Air would invite *me* out for ice cream," said Alexia, who used to be cool before Pee Air showed up.

"I can't believe you and Pee Air are going on a *date*!" said Emily.

"It's not a date," Andrea told the girls. "It's just ice cream."

"It's an ice cream date!" screamed Emily.

"Eeeeeek!"

"Don't be silly," said Andrea. "Pee Air and I are just friends."

"But he's a *boy*," Emily said. "So that means Pee Air is your *boy*friend!"

"Eeeeeek!"

Girls are weird.

The Greatest Idea in the History of the World

The I Scream Shop has the best ice cream in town. After school, me and the guys decided to go over there so we could spy on Andrea and Pee Air.

But we didn't want to go inside the I Scream Shop. We watched what was going on from across the street. It was cool. We were like secret agents. Neil got a pair of binoculars for his birthday, so he was our lookout as we hid in the bushes.

A few minutes after we arrived, Andrea and Pee Air showed up. We watched them go inside the I Scream Shop and sit in a booth near the window.

"What are they doing?" I asked Neil as he peered through the binoculars.

"It looks like he's giving her a card or something," Neil reported.

"It's probably some mushy love poem," I said. "It's his special valentine."

A few minutes passed.

"What are they doing *now*?" asked Ryan.

"He's giving her a stuffed animal," reported Neil. "She's giggling and acting all girly."

"A stuffed animal?" said Michael. "Where did he get a stuffed animal?"

"From Rent-A-Stuffed-Animal," I told

him. "You can rent anything."

"What are they doing *now*?" Michael asked a few minutes later.

"They're eating ice cream," Neil reported. "It looks like strawberry."

Strawberry?!

We were all bummed out. It didn't bother us that Pee Air was with Andrea. It bothered us that they were eating ice cream and we were hiding in the bushes across the street. And I love strawberry.

We were also bummed out because the next day was going to be Valentine's Day. We would have to make cards and read poems and talk about the *L* word all day. It was going to be *horrible*.

"Let's get out of here," I said to the guys.

"That Pee Air is one smooth operator," Michael said as we walked down the street.

"He probably *likes* the *L* word," I said.

"He loves love," said Neil. "I hate love."

"Pee Air thinks he is *so* great," Ryan complained.

"All the girls are making goo-goo eyes at him," said Ryan.

"Even Alexia likes him," said Michael, "and she used to be cool."

"We can't let that French pastry make us look bad," said Ryan.

We all laughed, because Ryan called Pee Air a French pastry.

"Yeah, we can't let that French pastry push us around," said Neil.

"That's right!" I said. "We should teach Pee Air a lesson."

"Yeah!" said Ryan. "What do you think we should–"

Ryan didn't get the chance to finish his sentence, because you'll never believe in a million hundred years who came running over to us.

It was Pee Air!

"Hey, guys!" he said.

"Why aren't you out eating ice cream with Andrea?" asked Michael. "She's your *special* valentine, right?"

"Andrea had to go to her . . . how do you say . . . clog-dancing class," Pee Air replied.* "Can I . . . hang out with you guys . . . for a while? Maybe I can practice my English with you."

I didn't want to be Pee Air's English teacher. I looked at Ryan. Ryan looked at Michael. Michael looked at Neil. Neil looked at me. I looked at Pee Air. And that's when I came up with the greatest idea in the history of the world.

"Sure, Pee Air," I said. "There are lots of English words and expressions that they don't teach you in school."

"Like what?" asked Pee Air.

"Like 'vomit,'" I said. "It means you have a good feeling. So if you really like somebody, you tell them that they make you vomit."

---

*Clog dancing is a kind of dancing that plumbers do.

"That's a good word!" said Pee Air. "Tell me another one."

The guys were all trying hard not to laugh.

"Well, in America, we call 'candy' 'snot,'" I told Pee Air. "People really like eating snot."

"Or finding snot in their pocket," added Ryan.

"Or getting snot in their lunch box," added Michael.

"I love eating snot," said Neil.

"I see," said Pee Air. "So I could ask a girl if she wants some of my snot?"

"Sure!" I said. "Girls love it when you share your snot with them."

We made up all kinds of other rude expressions and taught Pee Air how to say them. It was hilarious.

Maybe Valentine's Day won't be so bad after all.

Pee Air Is Out of Control

When I got to school the next morning, there were red and pink flowers and hearts all over the hallways. Ugh, disgusting!

I have bad news for you. A *real* heart doesn't look anything like those hearts they have on valentines. I saw a picture of a real heart once on TV. It was gross.

Mr. Granite wasn't in class yet. All the girls were giggling around Andrea, who was telling them about her big ice cream date with Pee Air.

"When we grow up," she said, "Pee Air and I will probably get married."

"Eeeeeek!" all the girls screamed.

"We're going to move to Paris and eat baguettes all day," said Andrea.

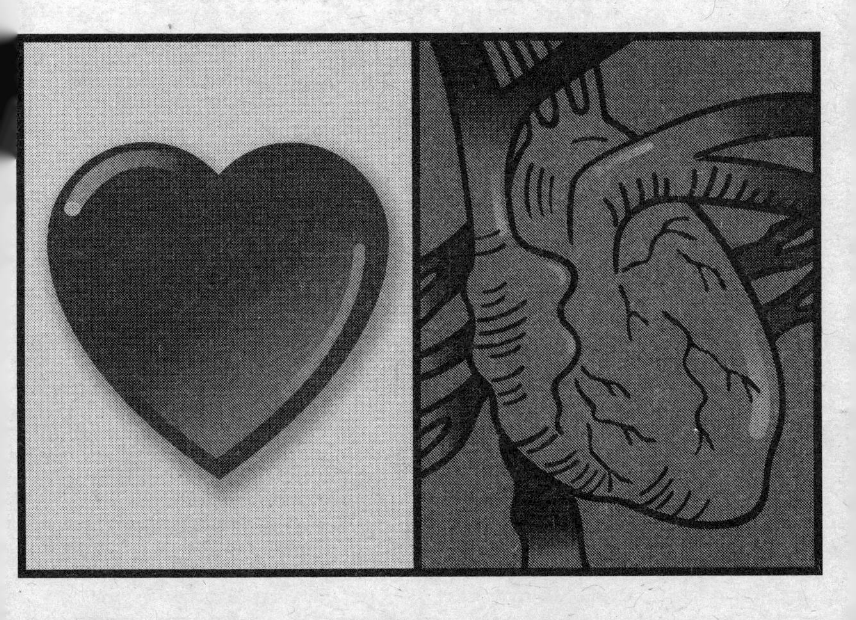

Pee Air walked in the doorway. He was wearing one of those weird beret thingies that people in France wear on their heads all the time. Nobody knows why. The girls lined up to get their hands kissed by Pee Air.

"Happy Valentine's Day, Pee Air!" said Andrea, holding her hand out.

"Andrea, my special valentine," said Pee Air. "I would like to give you a box full of snot . . . for Valentine's Day."

"What?!" Andrea said.

"I want to share my snot with you," Pee Air said. "I have some very fine snot . . . that I brought from France."

Andrea took a step backward. It looked

like she was going to faint.

"You brought snot from France?" she asked.

"Yes, the best snot in the world . . . is French snot," said Pee Air.

"They sell snot in stores there?" she asked.

"Oh yes, it is very expensive . . . and my family buys many boxes of snot. We store them in the . . . pantry."

Andrea sat down. She looked like she was going to be sick.

Emily held out her hand for Pee Air to kiss.

"Your eyes look like . . . giant toilets in the moonlight," said Pee Air as he kissed Emily's hand. "Your feet smell like . . . cabbages that have been left out in the sun too long. If I pick my nose . . . may I also pick yours? Your hair is so beautiful. Do you have head lice?"

Emily started crying and went running out of the room. What a crybaby! That's when Mr. Granite arrived.

"Happy Valentine's Day, everyone!" he said cheerfully.

Pee Air went over to Alexia and took her hand.

"Every snowflake is different . . . just like every piece of your dandruff. Your body odor is so pungent. Do you have fleas? Cockroaches must be happy . . . to live in your underwear."

"Pee Air!" said Mr. Granite. "What's gotten into you?"

Pee Air went over to Annette and took her hand.

"I apologize," he said. "May I taste your earwax? The perfume you are wearing . . . smells like elephant poop. Looking at your face . . . makes me vomit."

"Pee Air!" said Mr. Granite. "That is inappropriate language to use in school!"

Wow, Pee Air must have believed everything we told him about speaking English. That guy will fall for *anything*. Andrea looked like she might start crying.

"I thought I was your special valentine," she said to Pee Air.

"You are, Andrea," said Pee Air. "Your face is like . . . an unwashed armpit. I would like to sprinkle your toenail clippings . . . on my breakfast cereal."

"That's not nice to say!" Andrea said.

"I fart in your general direction," said Pee Air.

"That's it!" said Mr. Granite. "Pee Air, go to the principal's office!"

"What . . . what did I do?" asked Pee Air.

Me and the guys were falling all over each other trying not to laugh. This was going to be the best Valentine's Day *ever*!

8 This Means War

When Pee Air came back to class with Mr. Klutz, he looked really mad.

"Do you have anything to say to the girls in the class, Pee Air?" asked Mr. Klutz.

"I am sorry," Pee Air said, looking at the floor. He sat down in his seat. He looked at me and made a mean face.

"Maybe children are allowed to say

those kinds of things in France," said Mr. Granite, "but we don't talk like that here. Do you understand?"

"Oui," said Pee Air.

Ha-ha! In Pee Air's face! I guess I showed *him*. Maybe everybody will stop treating him like he's so perfect.

Mr. Klutz left. It was time for our Valentine's Day class party. My mom had given me little valentines to hand out to everybody in the class. So did all the other moms, so we all got lots of valentines. A few kids brought in cookies from home. Pee Air brought in a big box of French chocolate.

All right! It was about time we got some chocolate!

"Sweets for the sweet!" Pee Air said as he handed out his chocolates to everybody.

"I hope there's no snot in there," I whispered to Ryan.

Actually, Pee Air's French chocolate was *awesome.* It was *way* better than our chocolate. This was the best Valentine's Day *ever.* I had humiliated Pee Air, and I got to eat his chocolate, too. But that's when the weirdest thing in the history of the world happened. Pee Air stood up.

Well, that's not the weird part, because Pee Air stands up all the time. The weird part was what happened next.

"I would like to recite a poem . . . I wrote in English," he said. "It is for my special valentine."

Everybody looked at Andrea.

"Go ahead, Pee Air," said Mr. Granite. "We would love to hear your poem."

So Pee Air started reading. . . .

Your face is like the sun,
shining there so bright.
Your smile is like the sunrise
at the end of night.
Your eyes are like the ocean,
where fishes swim and play.
Your heart and mine are one,
on this, our Valentine's Day.

Pee Air sat down. Everybody started clapping. Andrea looked like she was going to cry tears of happiness. All the other girls were making goo-goo eyes at Pee Air.

"That was *beautiful*, Pee Air," said Mr. Granite. "I'm sorry I yelled at you."

Oh man! Everybody liked Pee Air again! It was like he never said all that stuff about snot and vomit and underwear and head

lice. Bummer in the summer!

At the end of the Valentine's Day party, while everybody was cleaning up, Pee Air pulled me aside.

"Teaching me those words was mean, A.J.," Pee Air said.

Well, he was right about that. It was mean. I didn't like Pee Air, and I didn't like him eating ice cream with Andrea.

"So is your face," I said to Pee Air.

If you don't know what to say to somebody, just say "So is your face." That's the first rule of being a kid.

"That is . . . as you say, the last straw!" said Pee Air.*

---

*People are always running out of straws. I don't see why they don't just buy an extra box of straws when they go shopping.

"What do straws have to do with anything?" I asked.

"This means war, A.J.," said Pee Air. "Andrea is *my* special valentine! Not yours."

"You can have her," I said. "I don't want her."

"Three o'clock," Pee Air said, pointing his finger at me. "In the playground."

"I'll *be* there, Pee Air!" I said.

Fighting is wrong. You should never fight. My parents tell me that all the time. My teachers tell me that, too.

But what was I supposed to do? Everybody knows what "Three o'clock, in the playground" means. Pee Air was challenging me to a fight. It would look really bad if I backed down.

For the rest of the day, I couldn't pay attention to what Mr. Granite was trying to teach us. All I could think about was the big fight after school. I've never been in a fight before. I didn't really know what to do.

"A.J., you're gonna be great," Ryan kept telling me. "Just keep your dukes up. That French pastry is going *down.*"

"You are The Man, A.J.," said Michael.

Finally, after a million hundred minutes, the clock on our classroom wall said it was three o'clock.

BRING! BRING! BRING!

Everybody grabbed their backpacks and rushed out to the playground. I mean *everybody*, even the fifth graders. I guess word got around that there was going to be a big fight after school.

When I got out to the playground, Pee Air was waiting for me. All the kids gathered in a big circle around us. Right behind me were my two best friends, Ryan and Michael.

I looked at Pee Air. Pee Air looked at me.

Then, suddenly, the crowd parted to let somebody through.

It was Andrea.

"Please don't fight, boys!" she said. "Violence never solved any problems."

What did violins have to do with anything?

"Back off, Andrea," I yelled to her. "This is between me and Pee Air."

"I think you mean Pee Air and me," said Andrea. "You should use correct grammar, Arlo."

"Quiet!" I shouted at her. "Can you

possibly be more boring?"

Andrea had distracted me. I had to focus my attention. I looked at Pee Air. Pee Air looked at me.

"A.J.," Pee Air said. "I challenge you . . . to a duel."

"Ooooooooooo!" everybody ooooooooed.

WHAT?!

I thought we were going to *fight.* Is duel a French word that means "fight"? I didn't know what he was talking about.

Michael and Ryan came over to me.

"I saw a duel in a movie once," Michael whispered. "You're supposed to throw a glove on the ground in front of Pee Air."

What?! Why would anybody throw a

glove on the ground? I didn't even have a glove. It wasn't even that cold outside. Who wears gloves to school when it's not cold out?

"Forget the glove," whispered Ryan. "Just keep your dukes up."

I turned back to face Pee Air again.

"Do you wish to apologize to me, A.J.?" Pee Air asked.

"What for?" I said.

"You have offended my honor."

"Oooooooooo!" everybody ooooooooed.

"I did not!" I said.

"Yes."

"No!"

"Oui!"

"Wee wee!"

Pee Air and I went back and forth like that for a while. Finally, Michael leaned over to me.

"Next," he whispered, "you're supposed to say, 'Choose your weapon.'"

"Weapon?" I asked. "I don't have any weapons. Nobody said anything about fighting with weapons."

"That's the rules, A.J.," said Michael. "Duels have rules."

"Choose your weapon, Pee Air," I said.

"Ooooooooo!"

Pee Air looked me in the eye.

"I choose . . . thumbs."

"Ooooooooo!"

So he wanted to thumb wrestle, eh? No problem. I've been in *plenty* of thumb wars in my time. And I'm a pretty good thumb warrior, if I do say so myself.

"I accept," I said.

"Oooooooooo!"

Pee Air put out his right hand. I put out my right hand. But you'll never believe who came running out to the playground at that moment.

It was Mr. Klutz and a bunch of the teachers!

"Okay, break it up, you two," shouted Mr. Klutz. "There will be *no* fighting on school property, especially not on Valentine's Day! This is supposed to be the day of tolerance and acceptance and *love*. Remember?"

Ugh, disgusting. He said the *L* word.

"They're not fighting," said Alexia. "They're going to have a thumb war."

"A *what*?" asked Mr. Klutz.

We had to explain to him what a thumb war was.* Can you believe that? Grown-ups don't know *anything*.

"Oh, well, I guess that's okay," said Mr. Klutz. "You may proceed. As long as there's no violence."

Why is everybody always talking about violins? And who would bring a violin

---

*Sheesh, do I have to show you everything? www.youtube.com/watch?v=Y17YCir0Ki8

to a thumb war? We didn't need musical accompaniment.

"Okay, A.J.," said Ryan. "This is for all the marbles."

"What do marbles have to do with anything?" I asked.

"Just beat him!" said Michael.

A hush fell over the crowd as Pee Air and I faced each other once again. There was electricity in the air.

Well, not really. If there had been electricity in the air, we all would have been electrocuted.

"May the better thumb win," I said to Pee Air.

Pee Air put out his right hand. I put out

my right hand. We grabbed hold of each other's hand. It was *very* dramatic.

Aren't you on pins and needles? Well, if you are, you should get off them and sit on a couch or something. Pins and needles hurt.

I put my thumb next to Pee Air's thumb. We started to move our thumbs back and forth. . . .

"One . . . two . . . three . . . four," we both said. "I declare a thumb war."

"Five . . . six . . . seven . . . eight," we both said. "I will make your knuckles ache."

"Four . . . three . . . two . . . one," we both said. "Who will be the strongest thumb?"

Pee Air moved his thumb left. I moved

my thumb left. Pee Air moved his thumb right. I moved my thumb right. It was very exciting!

"Get him, Pee Air!" somebody shouted.

"You can beat him, A.J.!"

Pee Air moved his thumb right. I moved my thumb right. Pee Air moved his thumb left. I moved my thumb left. We were frantically trying to get the upper hand. I mean, the upper thumb.

"You're going *down*, Pee Air!" I said.

"I don't *think* so!" Pee Air hissed back.

Everybody was yelling and cheering and freaking out. Even Mr. Klutz and the teachers! I almost had Pee Air's thumb down, but he moved it away just in time.

Then he almost had my thumb down, but I moved it away just in time.

The tension was unbearable.

And then, just before I was about to cover Pee Air's thumb with my thumb, he turned the tables on me and covered my thumb with *his* thumb.

"Noooooooooooo!" I shouted.

Pee Air's thumb was pressed down on top of my thumb hard. I couldn't move it.

"Victory is mine!" Pee Air shouted. *"Vive la France!"*

The Truth about Pee Air

Bummer in the summer!

Pee Air had beaten me fair and square at thumb wrestling. I thought I was gonna die. Everybody was hooting and hollering. My hand hurt. This was the worst thing to happen since National Poetry Month! I wanted to run away to Antarctica and go live with the penguins.

"Nice try, dude," said Ryan, putting his arm around me. "You gave it your best shot."

Michael gave me a thumbs-up, but then he must have realized that was a dumb thing to do, considering that I had just lost the thumb war.

"Hey, we should take A.J. out to the I Scream Shop," Michael said. "Maybe that will make him feel better."

Ice cream! All right! Michael should be in the gifted and talented program for coming up with that idea.

We walked a million hundred miles to the I Scream Shop. And when we opened the door, you'll never believe who we saw in there.

I'm not going to tell you.

Okay, okay, I'll tell you. It was Pee Air!

But you'll never believe who was with him.

I'm not going to tell you.

Okay, okay, I'll tell you. It was Alexia!

And they were both sitting at the same table! They had skateboards with them. That must have been how they got to the I Scream Shop before we did.

"Alexia!" I said. "What are *you* doing here with Pee Air?"

"Eating ice cream," she said. "What does it look like I'm doing here?"

"I invited Alexia . . . to join me to celebrate . . . my thumb war victory," said Pee Air.

Wow! So Andrea *wasn't* Pee Air's special valentine after all!

Maybe Alexia was Pee Air's special valentine. Or maybe Andrea was Pee Air's special valentine, but he was secretly going out for ice cream with Alexia behind Andrea's back. Or maybe Alexia was Pee

Air's special valentine, but he was secretly going out for ice cream with Andrea behind Alexia's back.

Valentine's Day was complicated. And it was about to get even *more* complicated. Because you'll never believe who came into the I Scream Shop at that moment.

I'm not going to tell you.

Okay, okay, I'll tell you. It was Andrea and Emily!

Andrea was holding the special valentine that Pee Air had given her.

Andrea looked at Pee Air. Pee Air looked at Andrea.

"Pee Air!" shouted Andrea.

"Andrea!" shouted Pee Air.

"What are you doing here with Alexia?" asked Andrea.

"Yeah," said Emily. "What are you doing here with Alexia?"

"They're eating ice cream," I said. "What does it *look* like they're doing?"

"I . . . I . . . I . . ." Pee Air didn't know what to say, at least not in English.

"Pee Air!" said Andrea. "You said *I* was your special valentine!"

"Yeah," said Emily. "You said Andrea was your special valentine!"

Andrea looked like she was going to cry. Pee Air looked like he wanted to be anywhere else in the world. He didn't know what to say. He didn't know what to do.

He had to think fast.

"In France, *all* the girls are special on Valentine's Day," he finally told Andrea. "There is plenty of love to go around. Don't you agree?"

"No!" shouted Andrea. "That's it! It's all over between us, Pee Air!"

Andrea ripped Pee Air's special valentine up into little pieces and threw them at Pee Air.

"Oh, snap!" said Ryan.

"I never want to see you again!" Andrea told Pee Air.

"Yeah!" said Emily. "Andrea never wants to see you again!"

It was the *awesomest*! You should have *been* there. And we got to see it live and in person.

"This is my worst Valentine's Day *ever*!" Andrea said. And then she stomped out of the I Scream Shop.

11 A Special Valentine

When I got to school the next morning, Pee Air was lugging a suitcase up the front steps.

"What's in the suitcase, Pee Air?" I asked. "Are you going to give us more stinky cheese?"

"No, I am going back home to France today," he told me. "But I wanted to say good-bye . . . to my new friends before I leave."

We got to our classroom, and Mr. Granite wasn't there yet. Pee Air went up to each girl in the class and kissed her hand. They were all giggling and making goo-goo eyes and getting his email address so they could stay in touch with him.

Finally, Pee Air went over to Andrea. She was standing in the corner like she was hiding or something.

"Your eyes . . . are like pools of water . . . in the moonlight," Pee Air said.

"Beat it, you two-timer!" shouted Andrea.

"Oh, snap!" said Ryan.

"Andrea, you will *always* be my special

valentine," Pee Air said as he bent down to kiss Andrea's hand. "Parting is such sweet sorrow–"

"Don't touch me!" she shouted as she slapped his hand away.

"Yeah," I told Pee Air, "get in your S car and go home."

"Au revoir," said Pee Air, whatever that means. And then he left.

Mr. Granite came into the classroom and told us to take our seats. I went to put my backpack in my cubby. When I got to my seat, Andrea came over to me. She was holding a valentine.

"Oh, Arlo," she said, "I've been thinking it over. You're *my* special valentine. You always will be."

"Ooooooooooo!" everybody ooooooooed.

That's when the most horrible thing in the history of the world happened. Before I could do anything, Andrea leaned over and *kissed me*!

Right on the *lips*!

"Ugh, disgusting!" I shouted, wiping my

face on my sleeve.

"Ooooo!" Ryan said. "Andrea kissed A.J.! They must be in *love*!"

"When are you and Andrea gonna get married?" asked Michael.

"Leave me alone!" I shouted at Andrea. "Now I have to go boil my face."

That's it. That's the last straw. I'm going to run away to Antarctica and go live with the penguins. Penguins don't go around kissing each other. I don't even think penguins *have* lips.

Now that Valentine's Day is over, maybe people will stop saying the *L* word all the time. Maybe we can exchange Andrea for

a video game system. Maybe French people will stop eating snails and throwing their clothes into puddles of water. Maybe Andrea will pick her nose with the same hand Pee Air kissed. Maybe I'll bring gloves to school in case I need to throw one on the ground. Maybe Napoleon will take his hand out of his shirt and get some ointment for that rash. Maybe we'll have a sword fight with baguettes. Maybe kids in France will stop spelling words wrong and bringing bears to school with them. Maybe people will stop talking about violins, running out of straws, and walking into doors all the time.

But it won't be easy!

My Weird School Special

Oh, Valentine, We've Lost Our Minds!

WEIRD EXTRAS!

- Professor A.J.'s History of Valentine's Day
- Fun Games and Weird Word Puzzles
- My Weird School Daze Trivia Questions
- The World of Dan Gutman Checklist

PROFESSOR A.J.'S HISTORY OF VALENTINE'S DAY

Greetings, My Weird School lovers!

Ewww, I said the *L* word! Disgusting!

Anyway, it's me, Professor A.J., the boy who knows everything that's worth knowing. I hope you have a great Valentine's Day with lots of chocolate and yummy stuff but no kissing, hugging, or any of that yucky stuff.

I think it's about time you learned something about Valentine's Day. For instance, did you know how this holiday started? Well, I'll tell you. . . .

It was way back in ancient times, when microwave popcorn hadn't even been invented yet. King Gerald the Third of Terdlandia was madly in love with a princess named Lucy. To prove his love for her, he decided to cut out his own heart and give it to her as a present. And that's what he did. Lucy was pretty impressed that Gerald loved her so much that he would cut his heart out. He dropped dead instantly, of course, but that was the first valentine, and that's why valentines are shaped like hearts today.

Okay, I totally made that whole thing up. King Gerald the Third? Terdlandia? Are you kidding? Man, I could tell you kids *anything*! I bet that if I told you the first valentine was sent by a guy named Val N. Tyne, you would buy it. Don't believe everything you read in a book. Especially a My Weird School book.

But here's some real *true* stuff about Valentine's Day that you probably don't know. . . .

FACT:

—Valentine's Day has been around for a really long time. It is rumored that February 14 was first declared "Valentine's Day" by Saint Pope Gelasius I in A.D. 496.

That's so long ago, it only has three numbers.

FACT:

—The first valentine card ever sent was written by a duke to his wife in 1415.

She opened the card and said, "What, no flowers?"

FACT:

—Hallmark has been creating Valentine's Day cards since 1916. Just six years earlier, an eighteen-year-old boy named Joyce Clyde Hall (yes, his name was Joyce. Get over it.) arrived in Kansas City, Missouri, with little more than two shoe boxes of postcards. He began selling the postcards. Eventually, Joyce and his brother Rollie formed Hall Brothers. They were printing their own greeting cards by 1915.

FACT:

—For Valentine's Day, more than 707 *million dollars* is spent on candy.

That's enough candy to feed . . . well, me and my friends for a few days anyway.

FACT:

—Americans buy nearly 189 *million* roses every Valentine's Day.

Then, a few days later, they're all dead. The roses, that is. Not the Americans.

FACT:

—According to Roman mythology, Venus, the goddess of the *L* word, adored red roses. That's why they are a symbol of the *L* word today.

Boy, it's good that she didn't adore earwax. That would have been weird.

FACT:

—Do you know those little candy hearts that have words on them? They were first made in 1866 by Daniel Chase. His brother Oliver started the NECCO company, and they make a hundred thousand pounds of Sweethearts every day. It is the bestselling Valentine's Day candy.

FACT:

—In the eighteenth and nineteenth centuries, British children would go from one house to the next on Valentine's Day, singing songs and asking for treats.

Hey, I think I'm gonna try that this year.

FACT:

—On the island nation of Tyrania, people celebrate Valentine's Day by waving chickens over their heads while singing "Zip-A-Dee-Doo-Dah."

Okay, that doesn't happen. And there is no nation named Tyrania. But it would be cool.

FACT:

—If you mix up the letters in VALENTINE'S DAY, you can spell EAT MY BOOGERS TODAY. Okay, that's not true. But you can spell SALTED NAY VINE, DEAL NASTY VEIN, INVADE SLAY TEN, and NAILED ANY VETS.

FACT:

—Kissing is gross, but people do a lot of it on Valentine's Day. The longest kiss in the history of the world took place on Valentine's Day in 2013, when Ekkachai and Laksana Tiranarat from Thailand kissed for 58 hours, 35 minutes, and 58 seconds.

Ugh. I think I'm gonna throw up.

FACT:

—Here's some other stuff that happened on February 14: Arizona became the forty-eighth state. The League of Women Voters was formed. Penicillin was discovered. Benjamin Franklin invented toothpaste.

Okay, not that last one.

I could tell you a lot more cool stuff about Valentine's Day, but I have to go make some microwave popcorn. Happy Valentine's Day!

–Professor A.J. (the prime minister of awesomeness)

LATE TO THE VALENTINE'S DATE

Directions: Help Andrea navigate this heart-shaped maze to get to Pierre, who's waiting for her at the I Scream Shop!

VALENTINE'S WORD HUNT

Directions: Can you find all ten Valentine's Day words hidden in this messy jumble of letters?

Z X H E A R T R L A C U P I D
E A N M L W F E H I H L X A Z
G C A N D Y A P I L O V E E M
D A K T D E L I G L C W G L H
H R O I F D L N A C O S B V C
U D P U W E B K O F L O W E R
K S T J T G Z Z S A A C D H B
D Q S V Y E Q L B H T C G E E
W E E R O S E S W E E K E R D
C D A T Q B A F I N V L C B P
Y B H C C D E C P B N O F C O
U V A L E N T I N E E C E A G
E V G W N W O L D A L I R G W
A N L F B I A G I R O D J S I
F E B R U A R Y L A I C A E R

HEART CHOCOLATE FLOWER VALENTINE LOVE

ROSES CANDY PINK CUPID FEBRUARY

A MATCH MADE IN HEAVEN

Directions: Each of the words or phrases in the list below matches one of the words in the circle. See if you can pair them up!

1. Cupid's → ________________
2. Red → ________________
3. Candy → ________________
4. Be → ________________
5. *X*s and → ________________
6. Violets are → ________________
7. Best → ________________
8. Secret → ________________

SECRET VALENTINE'S MESSAGES

Directions: Use this secret code to swap in letters below and help A.J. solve these Valentine's Day mysteries!

A	B	C	D	E	F	G	H	I
H	D	L	Q	C	K	W	E	J

J	K	L	M	N	O	P	Q	R
P	G	O	Y	B	N	T	R	F

S	T	U	V	W	X	Y	Z
X	Z	I	S	M	V	U	A

Who is Pierre's secret valentine?

___ ___ ___ ___ ___ ___

Z C H S U Z

What French dish consists of cooked snails?

___ ___ ___ ___ ___ ___ ___ ___

H V E Z Q K L P

DRAW YOUR OWN MY WEIRD SCHOOL CHARACTER!

PICTURE PERFECT

Directions: These two covers are almost a picture-perfect match. But there are a few key differences. Can you spot them? (Hint: there are ten.)

New York Times Bestselling Author
Dan Gutman
MY WEIRD SCHOOL SPECIAL
Oh, Valentine, We've Lost Our Mind!
EXTRAS GAMES! PUZZLES! AND MORE!
Pictures by Jim Paillot

MY WEIRDER SCHOOL TRIVIA

There's no way in a million hundred years you'll get all these answers right. So nah-nah-nah boo-boo on you! **Hint:** The answers all come from the My Weirder School series.

Q: WHAT DOES ALEXIA'S BLACK T-SHIRT SAY?

A: Led Zeppelin

Q: HOW MANY MUSCLES DO ELEPHANTS HAVE IN THEIR TRUNKS?

A: More than 40,000!

Q: WHAT IS MR. HARRISON'S NICKNAME?

A: Fritz (His first name is George.)

Q: WHO DUG THE HOLE IN THE BASEMENT OF ELLA MENTRY SCHOOL?

A: Digger the squirrel!

Q: WHAT NEWSPAPER DOES MRS. LILLY WORK FOR?

A: The *News Tribune Bulletin Inquirer*

Q: WHAT DOES MR. DOCKER DO WHEN HE'S NOT WORKING?

A: He goes running with his wife.

Q: WHAT IS THE *T* WORD THAT YOU SHOULD NEVER SAY AROUND MAYOR HUBBLE?

A: Taxes

Q: WHAT DOES MR. BURKE USE TO MAKE A BUSH SCULPTURE?

A: A chain saw

Q: WHAT DOES MS. BEARD, THE DIRECTOR, CALL EVERYONE SHE MEETS?

A: Chickie baby

Q: WHAT REALITY SHOW IS FILMING AT ELLA MENTRY SCHOOL?

A: *The Real Teachers of Ella Mentry*

Q: WHAT STUDENT OFFICE DOES A.J. RUN FOR?

A: Class president

Q: WHO MODERATES THE ELECTION DEBATE BETWEEN A.J. AND ANDREA?

A: Mrs. Roopy, the librarian

Q: ACCORDING TO MR. KLUTZ, WHAT DOES BOGS STAND FOR?

A: Behave or Get Suspended

Q: WHAT IS MISS KRAFT'S MAGICIAN NAME?

A: The Great Kraftini

Q: WHERE DOES A.J. SAY FREEDOM OF SPEECH COMES FROM?

A: Your mouth

Q: WHO INVENTED THE FIRST TOILET BOWL YOU COULD FLUSH?

A: John Harrington, in 1596

Q: WHAT DO PEOPLE CALL ALEXIA'S MOM, MS. SUE?

A: Queen of Cupcakes

Q: WHO STEALS THE MONEY FROM THE FUND-RAISING CARNIVAL?

A: Mayor Hubble

Q: WHAT DOES MR. JACK DRIVE?

A: A big, black motorcycle

Q: WHAT DOES ANDREA DO TO THE BEAR THAT INVADES ELLA MENTRY SCHOOL?

A: She karate chops it!

ANSWER KEY

LATE TO THE VALENTINE'S DATE

VALENTINE'S WORD HUNT

Z X H E A R T R L A C U P I D
E A N M L W F E H I H L X A Z
G C A N D Y A P I L O V E E M
D A K T D E L I G L C W G L H
H R O I F D L N A C O S B V C
U D P U W E B K O F L O W E R
K S T J T G Z Z S A A C D H B
D Q S V Y E Q L B H T C G E E
W E E R O S E S W E E K E R D
C D A T Q B A F I N V L C B P
Y B H C C D E C P B N O F C O
U V A L E N T I N E E C E A G
E V G W N W O L D A L I R G W
A N L F B I A G I R O D J S I
F E B R U A R Y L A I C A E R

A MATCH MADE IN HEAVEN

1. Cupid's → **ARROW**
2. Red → **ROSES**
3. Candy → **HEARTS**
4. Be → **MINE**
5. *X*s and → **Os**
6. Violets are → **BLUE**
7. Best → **FRIENDS**
8. Secret → **ADMIRER**

SECRET VALENTINE'S MESSAGES

Who is Pierre's secret valentine?

A L E X I A

What French dish consists of cooked snails?

E S C A R G O T

PICTURE PERFECT

THE WORLD OF DAN GUTMAN CHECKLIST

MY WEIRD SCHOOL

☐ ☐ ☐ ☐

Miss Small Is off the Wall!
Dan Gutman
Mr. Hynde Is Out of His Mind!
Pictures by Jim Paillot
Dan Gutman
Mrs. Cooney Is Loony!
Pictures by Jim Paillot
Dan Gutman
Ms. LaGrange Is Strange!
Pictures by Jim Paillot
Dan Gutman
Miss Lazar Is Bizarre!
Pictures by Jim Paillot
Dan Gutman
Mr. Docker Is off His Rocker!
Pictures by Jim Paillot
Dan Gutman
Mrs. Kormel Is Not Normal!
Pictures by Jim Paillot
Dan Gutman
Ms. Todd Is Odd!
Dan Gutman
Mrs. Patty Is Batty!
Pictures by Jim Paillot
Dan Gutman
Miss Holly Is Too Jolly!
Mr. Macky Is Wacky!
Dan Gutman
Ms. Coco Is Loco!
Pictures by Jim Paillot

Dan Gutman
Miss Suki Is Kooky!
Jim Paillot

Dan Gutman
Mrs. Yonkers Is Bonkers!
Jim Paillot

Dan Gutman
Dr. Carbles Is Losing His Marbles!
Jim Paillot

Dan Gutman
Mr. Louie Is Screwy!
Jim Paillot

Dan Gutman
Ms. Krup Cracks Me Up!
Jim Paillot

MY WEIRD SCHOOL DAZE

Dan Gutman
Mrs. Dole Is Out of Control!
Jim Paillot

Dan Gutman
Mr. Sunny Is Funny!
Jim Paillot

Dan Gutman
Mr. Granite Is from Another Planet!
Jim Paillot

Dan Gutman
Coach Hyatt Is a Riot!
Jim Paillot

Officer Spence Makes No Sense!
Jim Paillot

Dan Gutman
Mrs. Jafee Is Daffy!

Dr. Brad Has Gone Mad!

Miss Laney Is Zany!
Jim Paillot

MY WEIRDER SCHOOL

MY WEIRD SCHOOL SPECIAL

THE GENIUS FILES